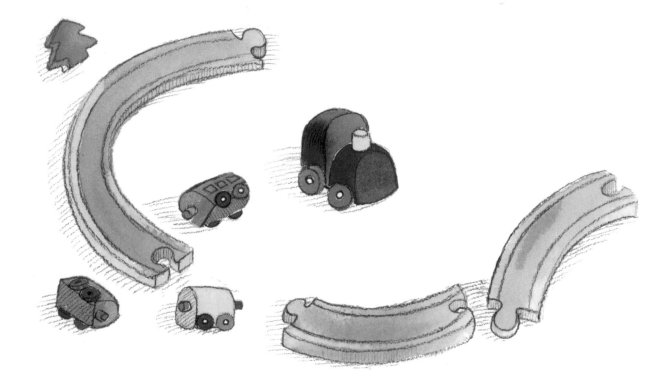

This edition published by Parragon Books Ltd in 2014

Parragon Books Ltd
Chartist House
15–17 Trim Street
Bath BA1 1HA, UK
www.parragon.com

Written by David Bedford
Edited by Laura Baker
Production by Jonathan Wakeham

Illustrated by Susie Poole
Designed by Alex Dimond and Duck Egg Blue

ISBN 978-1-4723-6703-7

Printed in China

You're a **BIG** Brother

Bath · New York · Cologne · Melbourne · Delhi
Hong Kong · Shenzhen · Singapore · Amsterdam

You're going to be a big brother!
Hooray! How lucky are you?

Babies LOVE their big brothers

and the clever things that they do.

Babies can SMELL...

and pull hair as well...

so watch out and hold on to your nose!

Babies make mums and dads busy –
they won't just be caring for you.

But now that you're a big brother,
it's fun sharing with somebody new.

Babies don't do much to start with,

so just quietly show them your toys.

They can't dance or sing,

but they like
to join in...

by making a gurgling noise!

Babies learn lots from big brothers,
so teach them all you can do:

Share and

take care...

be baby's best friend,

and they'll be amazing...

just like YOU!